NINARPHAY TALES
VOLUME V AND VI

Vol V: The Three Sages and the Sword of Light
Vol VI: The Four Crowns

LEON LOWE

AuthorHouse™ UK
1663 Liberty Drive
Bloomington, IN 47403 USA
www.authorhouse.co.uk
UK TFN: 0800 0148641 (Toll Free inside the UK)
UK Local: 02036 956322 (+44 20 3695 6322 from outside the UK)

Because of the dynamic nature of the Internet, any web addresses or links contained in this book may have changed
since publication and may no longer be valid. The views expressed in this work are solely those of the author and do
not necessarily reflect the views of the publisher, and the publisher hereby disclaims any responsibility for them.

Any people depicted in stock imagery provided by Getty Images are models,
and such images are being used for illustrative purposes only.
Certain stock imagery © Getty Images.

This book is printed on acid-free paper.

ISBN: 978-1-7283-7967-8 (sc)
ISBN: 978-1-7283-7968-5 (e)

Library of Congress Control Number: 2022924111

Print information available on the last page.

Published by AuthorHouse 12/29/2022

authorHOUSE®

CONTENTS

NINARPHAY TALES VOL. V

THE THREE SAGES AND

THE SWORD OF LIGHT

THE SUMMONED SAGES

In Ninarphay, a short time after the battle for the nine Talismans, two High Lord Sages are summoned to appear before the Grand Lord Reaper and the Queen Witch.

Our journey began twenty years ago when the Ice Witch and Tarot King were in study to become Sages.

They were learning about Prophecy Scrolls under the tutorship of Elf Principal Hawk in the Elf Lands Education City.

It was their final day before graduation, and they had jointly requested the last tutorial on Prophecy before their graduation.

Principal Hawk puts a Blank Prophecy Scroll in a Black Water Fountain. He pours in some Ink and then utters an Incantation, "prophecy in east, north, south, and west reveal to me the state of Ninarphay before I rest!" He is called away and tells his two students, "This is the last time you'll see me for a while. I must be going, but don't forget to follow the Prophecy Scrolls faithfully and remember the ways of Ninarphay!" The Grand Elf leaves the room, and the two Ninarphaians read the Scroll of Prophecy.

The Scroll reads, 'twenty years from now in the Realm of Ninarphay, a battle looms that may see the downfall of this once prosperous and harmonious realm. Devil Lord Satoi, one of the seven enemies of Ninarphay, shall return to destroy his antithesis.

Satoi shall slice through the Land with his Sword of Light like a

Knife through Butter. The only way to stop this Devil Lord is to retrieve the Sword of Light and trap Satoi forever in the Dark Moon Tower.

Conjure the Sword, use Satoi's Ruby, which can be found only in the Caves of Ninarphays Nymph Lands.

Partake in a ritual in the Banshee Lands, retrieve Satoi's Armour from the Reaper Lands and then finally Conjure the Sword by placing the Prophecy Scrolls in a Magic Fountain in the Goblin Lands.

They take the Scroll out of the Fountain, and the Ice Witch folds it into a Special Book.

The Ice Witch tells the Tarot King, "we must protect the scroll. I must keep the realm of Ninarphay safe and peaceful! The Tarot King responds, "I am a Regent, and I must defend Ninarphay from destruction"!

C H A P T E R 2

SEARCH FOR THE PRESTIGIOUS JEWEL

They fly to the Banshee Lands on the back of the Ice Witch Sage's Dragon.

They land at the border of the Banshee Lands and begin their search for the jewel in the Cave.

The Banshee Lands are Rich in hoarded Jewels of Power and Prestige, and many of the Jewels have Magic qualities and specialities.

Jewels of Prestige and Power are what the Banshee Lands are famous for, but the two Sages were indeed looking for a particular type of Jewel.

They arrive at the Border and leave their Dragon in the Care of a Boarder Clerk. They wander through the first town in the Banshee Lands until they come to a Jeweller.

They search for the Shop Clerk but find that the Shop is empty. The two Sages come across a mesmerising glowing Emerald. They pick it up, and it begins to glow.

Suddenly the Shop Clerk appears from nowhere and exclaims, "don't move a muscle"!

The shop clerk turns to them snatching the Jewel from their Hands and placing the Jewel back in its rightful Place. She tells them, "The Jewel is rare and has the power to grant wishes, but there is a catch to each wish you make. If you make a wish out of wanting, it curses, but if you indeed make a wish out of need, it blesses you.

Now, what can I do for you?" The Tarot King Sage tells the Clerk, "I am in search of Satoi's Ruby."

The clerk informs them. "the ruby is in the caves of the banshee lands with gargoyle guardians looking over it".

"A prophecy Scroll has been conjured and has revealed that twenty years after the disappearance of all young Ninarpahiens, a worse invasion will occur.

In this invasion, the Devil Lord Satoi will invade and destroy Ninarphay forever".

We have twenty years to ensure we find all three relics. Can you help?" The Banshee clerk reaches for the Emerald and conjures a Map and a Note Paper with a name on it.

She tells the two Sages, "Follow this Map. It leads you to a Tavern. Ask for the name on the Tavern, and the banshee will guide you to the catacombs where I believe this Jewel resides. They leave for the Tavern and spend two days and two nights on foot searching for it.

They soon come to the Tavern and enter. They ask for the name on the Note. "Is there a Murrell in here?" A banshee quickly jumps and draws her Sword.

She holds it to them and says, "Who are you? Speak!" the Ice Witch tells her, "don't be alarmed; we are just here in search of a guide. Can you help us?" The Tarot King Sage steps in, saying, "we are in search of the catacombs. We are Sages from the Reaper and Witch Lands. Can you please help us?" The banshee withdraws her weapon and says, "It will cost five Gold Coins if you want me to lead you into the Catacombs." The Ice Witch Sage tips out ten Gold Coins and places them in her hand, saying, "we'll pay you double"! Murrell says to them, "Let's be on our way. "They journey into the Mountains and then into the Catacombs. They use the Map to identify the Path through the Catacombs and the Scroll to identify the Ruby.

After two weeks of searching, they finally come to a Den inside the Catacombs inside a Cave.

They enter and begin searching for the jewel. They soon uncover the final Place, a Chest with many Rubies. They check through until they come to the most identical Ruby.

For each Ruby that they touched, Evil Gargoyles appeared. They put the correct Ruby in their Satchel, and as they turn around, thirty Evil Gargoyles Guardians of the leading Ruby halt them.

The Gargoyles tell them, "we are Servants of Satoi and have been sent to Guard his Ruby; you cannot leave with it." The Tarot King Sage tells them, "too bad!" Then two Sages begin to fight.

Once they defeat the thirty Guardian Gargoyles of the Catacomb, the Ruby glows and levitates in Mid-Air. It spins and emanates a Great light spinning uncontrollably. It soon materialises another Gargoyle.

Grand Sage Gargoyle Gayla appears and tells the two sages, "Thank you for releasing me from my Prison.

I am the Custodian of the Jewel and once Prisoner Grand Sage Guardian Gayla. I was imprisoned in that Jewel by Satoi himself. Your reward for freeing me is my Devotion and service to your cause!" The Tarot King tells her, "Grand Sage Gayla Satoi is plotting on us, and in twenty years, he will return to Ninarphay to conquer our Realm.

Will you journey with us to emanate his Sword of Light twenty years from now?" Gayla says, "I shall." Grand Sage Gayla approaches them with her massive Wings and Strong Frame. She takes the Jewel and tells them. "Conjure, and I will charge the Jewel; once we place it on the Parchment, it will lead us to the Relics." They conjure a Prophecy Scroll, which only forms for a few seconds. Grand Sage Gayla tells them, "Satoi must have put a protective barrier around it.

This level of Magic will take years to unravel." Five years later, Grand Sage Gayla, Ice Witch Sage and Tarot King Sage are in their Sage Villa trying to conjure up Prophecy Spells. Finally, Grand Sage Gayla conjures the Prophecy Scroll, which lasts for a long time.

CHAPTER 3

THE THREE SAGES AND THE SACRED CATHEDRAL

She calls over the Ice Witch Sage and the Tarot King Sage.

They come rushing in with the Jewel and Place it at the Centre of the Scroll. The Scroll soon reads, "the Reaper Lands Magma Mountain." A Map also begins inscribing on the Parchment, and the three Sages make their way to the Magma Mountains.

Ice Witch Sage and Tarot King Sage fly on the back of the Ice Witches' Dragon whilst Grand Sage Gayla uses her Wings and flies beside them.

Satoi is sitting in his Helios Realm Dwelling. He watches them through his seeing Fountain, then turns to his Servant and says, "it seems as though they're preparing for battle. It's a shame I am imprisoned in the Void and cannot leave." The image fades, and Satoi can no longer see the going on in Ninarphay.

The three Sages arrive at the Top of the Mountain and see a Cathedral Entrance. They enter the Cathedral and walk through it until they enter an Armoury.

They search around the Armour until Gayla pulls a Hammer on the Wall and opens up a Secret Entrance. A spiral Staircase appears, and the three Sages walk down it carefully and slowly, ensuring they don't drop.

The Staircase is steep without a side Bannister to rely on for support. They get down and come to a Suit of Armour.

They Place the Jewel in the Centre of the Armour. The Sword of Light summoned only light and has yet to be entirely installed into the Realm of Ninarphay.

Gayla tells them, "We must return to another Time; the Magic of Ninarphay won't allow a Weapon from The Void to enter. It will take a long Time." The three Sages leave and return fifteen years later.

The Sword of Light materialises and drops into a Special Plinth with Magic Markings that act as a barrier to the Evil Magic contained within the Sword.

The next day the three Sages are called a summons to meet with the Grand Lord Reaper and the Queen Witch.

They are given Food and Drink and meet with the Grand Hierarchy of Ninarphay.

They are then called to the Grand Hall, where the two Grand Lords sit, and the Summit begins. Satoi enters the So Above So Below Temple in his Palace in the Realm of The Void.

A Transzalore General knocks on his Celestial Doors, which he accesses from a Valley in Transzalore using multiple Spells and Incarnations.

Satoi sends his Servant to answer the Door. Satoi returns to his Throne Room, and Dark Lord Zenith tells him, "Lord Satoi, for the past twenty years, I have been in search of my Four Crowns that were stolen from me but have not been able to retrieve them. I am asking for your help to get them back to Ninarphay and invade Ninarphay as we did twenty years ago." Satoi responds to Dark Lord Zenith, saying, "I will be obliged, but first, I must find my Armour and Sword.

The Problem is I was looking for them, but they weren't there, so I will have to go to Ninarphay and retrieve them." Satoi throws a Jewel into his all-seeing Fountain and utters the Incantation, "So Above, So Below allow me to where I must go." Satoi's Void Gates open, and he walks into Ninarphay.

C H A P T E R   4

NINARPHAYS FOUNDER

He appears in Ninarphay Forest in the Griffin Lands and begins his journey. Satoi walks to the Border of the Griffin Lands and is immediately confronted by the Grand Griffin Eohdor and the Great Sprite Ladel.

Ladel is carrying her Sword across a Veil which is covering an Instrument. Eohdor says to Satoi, "you are not welcome in these Lands return at once, or you will be sorry." Satoi holds his hands in front of him, sticks out his Fingers, and says, "Dark Art Necromancy Arises Minions." twelve Skeletons arise from the ground with Swords and Axes, then attack Ladel and Eohdor. Eohdor says to Ladel, "Ladel stay back and Protect the Instrument." Eohdor battles long and hard, soon defeating the Necromancers.

Satoi says to Eohdor, "give up; you're not Powerful enough to defeat me on your own." Eohdor exclaims to Ladel, "now, Ladel!" Ladel throws the magical Veil over Satoi and the magical Veil covers Satoi's body revealing his Wrist Watch.

Beneath the Veil is an Hour Glass with glowing specks of light instead of sand. She throws the particles of light on the Timepiece, and it smashes.

The specks of light settle into the Timepiece and turn Black. Satoi deflects the Veil, soon defeating Ladel. Satoi continues his journey through Ninarphay.

Satoi arrives at a Clairvoyant House and enters the Premises. Meanwhile, at the summit, the Grand Lord Reaper and the Queen Witch take their Seats in the Hall, and the conference begins.

Queen Witch says, "well done, you have retrieved the Sword of light now. Place the Sword on the Plinth.

The Barrier Spells holding the Sword is our most powerful asset designed for Weapons such as the Sword of light with the Sword being held by Ninarphay, we are sure to win the ensuing battles."

The Grand Reaper Lord says, "well done, you are some of the Greatest Sages in the Land, and with your abilities, I would expect nothing less." The Grand Reaper Lord and the Queen Witch lean in and say at the same time together, "was it difficult." The Ice Witch Sage Tabitha says, "we encountered a few problems, but in the end, these problems were Beneficial to our cause."

The Tarot Sage King Cedric says, "we rescued Grand Gargoyle Sage Gayla from her Relic Prison. She hasn't told us all we know about herself, but she helped us get this far, so I Trust her."

The Queen Witch looks around at Grand Gargoyle Gayla and says, "you're from Devounouir, aren't you."

Gayla levitates out of her chair. A wind blows through the great hall. Gayla glows a Beam of light emanating from her Body.

The High Lords overlooking the summit each draw for the Weapons in anticipation. The Queen Witch signals to them to stand down.

Gayla Chants in Gargoyle Tongue before saying to Queen Witch, "Thank you for freeing me from the Curse, Queen Witch. You had broken the Spell before the fall of Devounouir. I was a Grand Sage, a Hierarchy level conferred higher than a Grand Lord of Ninarphay.

CHAPTER 5

THE FALL OF DEVOUNOUIR

"Twenty years ago, before the fall of Ninarphay and Devounouir. Transzalore, Narnyae and The Void, the realm of Powerful Evil Lords, conspired to bring down Devounouir to take down Ninarphay.

They choose to take down Devounouir for one reason and one reason alone. The Hierarchy of Devounouir were inclined to save the Harmony of Ninarphay and Ninarphay itself at all costs.

We had no problems with Transzalore and Narnyae, but the Evil Lords of The Void were too much for us.

We were overwhelmed, and to ensure our demise, they used Amulets, Scribes, Plinths, Relics, Scrolls and Magical Ornaments for every last ounce of the Love realm Devounouir".

"where is and what is Devounouir," the tarot king asks. "Can you tell me, have you heard anything of Devounouir?"

The Queen Witch tells her, "I'm sorry Devounouir has disappeared. Every trace of Devounouir is gone, even the telluric Plane and Magic Sphere.

There is no trace of Devounouir; Devounouir is no more. You are the first Devounourian I have seen in twenty-one years." Gayla asks, "what about the Devounourian creators of this land, Mylya, Enya and Horatia?

Have you heard from them?" Queen Witch says I'm afraid they disappeared with Devounouir." Gayla cries, "stop their Evil kin from The Void.

How can they be so Evil." the Grand Lord Reaper says, "The Seven Immortals who created this Land will return one day."

Back to the Sword. This Sword we have captured has the Power to alter Minds and cut through anything that includes Magic.

Now that we have the Sword, we can prepare for the coming of the Evil Lord Satoi. Prepare the Spells." Several High Lords walk to the Centre of the Room and begin painting on the Centre of the Floor.

They paint a Hexagon around a Pentagon star overlapping in a Circle of Rosemary. The Queen Witch stands over it and turns it Invisible.

The Queen Witch says to the High Lords and Sages at the summit, "Satoi has arrived in Ninarphay, and it's believed he will arrive here before sundown." High Lord Twill, the

Banshee Princess of the Witch Lands, says. "we shall be well prepared for him, my Queen!" meanwhile, in the Griffin Lands.

Five Fairies fly from the Grand Griffin's Sky Castle with Healing.

Kits. Satoi enters a Town in the Griffin Lands renowned for its Psychics and Clairvoyant Culture.

Satoi searches for the Psychic House, most likely to help him. He stops for a while and has a Meal at a Diner. Meanwhile, back at Ninarphay Forest.

The Grand Griffin Eohdor and the Great Sprite Ladel are getting healed by the Fairies. Eohdor turns to Ladel and says, "it's Time, Ladel; the invasion is almost upon us; after we heal, you must find those Ninarphaians.

Your quest to save Ninarphay begins." meanwhile, Satoi finishes his Meal and restarts his journey through the Town to find a Clairvoyant.

He comes to a Clairvoyant House, stops and enters. Inside, the interiors are Wooden and straightforward yet have Elegance to them.

He wonders through and doesn't see anyone. He comes to the Back of the House and enters the Library. He sees a Dwarf lady reaching for a Book.

She says to him, "what do you want?" Satoi tells her, "I am searching for something that belongs to me." the Dwarf tells Satoi, "I can't help you. The magic you are seeking is too powerful for me." Satoi pulls out a Satchel and pours Gold Coins into his Hand.

The Dwarf lady runs over and counts them, saying, "Okay, come with me." she takes him into the Room next Door, where a Crystal Ball is on a circular Table on top of the Red Cloth. They sit by the Table and put their Hands on the Crystal Ball.

She channels a Psychic Link to the Sword, but suddenly the Psychic Link catapults her across the room, slamming her into the Wall. She staggers to her feet, panting and wheezing, then tells Satoi, "the answers you seek are on the Magma Mountains in the Reaper Lands." Satoi opens his Helios Gate and walks through it.

Satoi appears on Magma Mountain. Satoi walks into the Cathedral and travels through it until he comes to the Armoury; as he enters the Armoury, the High Lords throw Rosemary on him, which sticks to his Clothes.

Satoi quickly battles them, and after a minute, they are soon defeated. Sneezing heavily, Satoi opens the Secret Panel and walks down the Spiral Staircase into the hidden Armoury. He searches for his Sword of light Armour and finds nothing.

Satoi bites his Finger and summons a Crystal Skull telling the Crystal Skull to find his Armour. The Crystal Skull glows and then turns to him, saying, "it is not only the Sword of light that has gone, but they have taken the Red Jewel Gayla and locked a Pantheon level Barrier Spell over their Location.

Not even the Void Lord Satoi can find them." Satoi then Crushes the Skull in his Palm, and the Skull disappears.

Satoi then bites his Finger and recites a Mantra, "elfin spirits of the east, elfin spirits of the west, elfin spirits of the north, elfin spirits of the south, find my own and show me now." three tracking Spirits then appear and say to Satoi in unison, "at your service Master." Satoi says to them, "find my Armour Jewel and Sword." they say, "yes, Master!" they quickly fly off. They zip through the nine Lands of Ninarphay, first appearing in the Griffin Lands overseeing the Grand Griffins Castle, then in the Grand Tengu's Pavilion, then flashing to the Blue Turtle's Lair and then they finally stop in the Reaper Lands.

They then return to Satoi to tell him the tracks have gone cold in the Reaper Lands. They say, "they began their initial search twenty years ago.

Their final search ended here. The trail ended in the Reaper Lands." Satoi retracts the three Spirits and opens Void Gate into the Reaper Lands. In the Grand Reaper Summit Hall, Great Goblin Remy enters the Hall with a Scroll Book, Ink, and Feather Pen.

He exclaims to the Grand Lord Reaper and Queen Witch at the end of the one-Acre Grand Summit Hall, "the Scroll, the Magic Ink and the Feather Pen are now ready to write the Memoirs." the Grand Reaper says, "Enter and sit at a table close to the Three Sages." the Grand Reaper then says to the Three Sages, "now that you have the Sword and Armour tell us how you came about finding them.

18

Start from the beginning." the Ice Witch Sage begins by telling them, "it all started twenty years ago when the Tarot King and I were merely High Lords.

We studied at the conjure Academy in the Elf Lands by Great Elf Solomay, who taught us how to progress from High Lord status to Sage status.

We came across a Spell to conjure Prophecy Spells. It took us days to finally perfect the conjuration of a Sacred Hidden Prophecy Scroll.

The Prophecy Scroll claimed that twenty years from then, Satoi shall invade Ninarphay for the second time and this time, he will not just kidnap the Young and mane their Parents, but he will claim the Land of Ninarphay, and it shall be like Void with the grind of his Sword of light and So Above So Below Armour.

The Prophecy Scroll also detailed the Cathedral of the Above Below Armoury Shrine and how a Grand Sage crafted the Shrine to one day be able to claim Evil Artefacts of Satoi if he should ever invade again." the Tarot King steps forward and tells more of the story. "we then began our quest to find the Sword of light.

The Scroll specified that we must find the Armour and the Jewel then, and only then will we have the power to summon the Sword.

We first sought Satoi's Red Jewel in the Banshee Lands, where imprisoned Mystical Gargoyles, very rare in Ninarphay, were guarding it.

We thought about them long and hard, but soon the Power of two Sages overpowered the Guardian Gargoyles, considered the most Powerful Guardians.

Once we retrieved, an Enchantment was released, and so too was Grand Sage Gayla. A Pantheon classed Sage of the now Mythical Devounouir. It was believed that Devounouir was lost to the forces of The Void twenty-one years ago.

She came with us on our Quest." Grand Sage Gayla then steps forward and gives her account. She says to the Ninarphaians at the Summit, "I used the Red Jewel to chart a Map to the Armour, and when we got there, we came to a Hidden Armoury; after excavating, we saw that it was the So Above So Below Armoury Shrine of Satoi.

We placed the Jewel into the Heart of the Armour and summoned the Sword. That is our story." A High Lord enters the Summit Hall in a panic and says! "my Grand Lords Satoi is finally here"! The Grand Lord Reaper and Queen Witch arise to their Feet. The High Lords and Sages ready their Weapons.

CHAPTER 6

SATOI'S SAGE BATTLE

The Queen Witch says to the High Lords and Sages in the Grand Hall. He is coming.

Gayla, Ice Witch and Tarot King shift closer to the Grand Lord Reaper and Queen Witch. Satoi is standing outside up in a Tree, looking through a Stain Glassed Window from up High.

He jumps to the Ground and enters the Hall. There is a Great Barrier Spell around the Domain. Satoi finds it impossible to join, so he uses his Void Gate.

Satoi goes to rewind time on his Sundial, but it doesn't work. A Black Glue substance keeps it from moving.

The High Lords then uncover the sunlight from the Roof of the Domain, which directly shines on Satoi.

The Queen Witch begins reciting a Mantra. "So Above, So Below may the harmonies of Nature and nurture take this Beast Back Below.

Back to his Void Home. Glory Ninarphay light and Love free us from this Evil Spirit which wishes us the unjust!" lights grow from the Hexagram Pentagram Seal Symbol on the Floor.

The Lock on the Void Gate breaks open, and the Locks form Locks on Locks. The Grand Reaper Lord shouts. "Tarot King now." the Tarot King places two Tarot Cards on either Side of the Symbol Circle.

Just one Side on the Edge. He places a Black Moon Tarot Card on the Southern Tip and a Dark Tower Card on the Northern Tip and says. "Black Moon of the South, may your tidal influences keep the above and below.

Dark Tower of the North, may your night be permanent, and Tower Walls trap this Evil Spirit in your Prison." the Tarot Cards glow and activate.

The Queen Witch finishes her Mantra. "never return to this Place as Ninarphay is no Place for The Void Lords." the Void Gates swallow up Satoi, and he is transported to the Black Moon, Dark Tower Prison of The Void. The three Sages, the Queen Witch and the Grand Reaper Lord, are enchanted with him.

The Queen Witch says, "we have not got very long." A Sand Dune appears and shows they only have ten minutes to Seal Satoi in the Dark Tower.

Twenty minutes before The Void Gates closes permanently with no chance of escape for anyone.

The five drag Satoi to the Spellbound Satoi to the top of the Tower. Ravens fly past them, and they cross abandoned forms of torture.

They get to the top floor, but as they are about to lock up Satoi, he wakes up, and a battle commences to get him through the Door.

The Power of two Grand Lords and three Sages soon sees Satoi locked in the Tower. Queen Witch incites a Mantra and locks Satoi up in the Tower.

They have five minutes left on the hourglass to escape the Realm. Gayla says to them, "no time, we must get to the Top of the Tower." they race to the Top of the Tower and then grab Gayla's Lasso.

Directly ahead in The Void Gate, which is closing. She flies them through the Domain, watching as The Void Gates begin closing and the Sand Dunes drip their last Sand.

They fly through The Void Gate; as they fly through and enter the Grand Summit Hall, The Void Gate slams shut locks and disappear into the Hexagram Pentagram Symbol.

The five Ninarphaians lying on the Floor are relieved, and a loud cheer is heard through the Hall. The morning arrives, and the Sages are given commendations.

The end

CONTENTS

NINARPHAY TALES VOL VI

THE FOUR CROWNS

CHAPTER 1

THE FOUR CROWNS PLEA

The four Monarchs are in their Prison Realm, which resembles the Forest of Ninarphay. They each share a Castle with four Throne Rooms. The Realm is an Autumn Purgatory identical to the Grand Griffins Kingdom Land. Tresel walks into the Castle from outside and asks Nivea, "did you make it out of the Forest?" Nivea turns to her and says, "it was the same as usual, you walk to the End of the Forest, and as you exit, you begin again at the beginning." Sastia barges in and exclaims to the other three Monarchs. "you three come immediately to the sealing Fountain." the four Monarchs run to the sealing Fountain and look inside it. "the invasions are beginning; let's watch." the four Monarchs peer through the Fountain and watch Ladel and Eohdor in the Sky Castle. Healers are in the infirmary tending to Eohdor and Ladel. The healers tell them, "both of your wounds have been fully healed, and you may be discharged." Eohdor asks, "are we fit for battle?" the healer tells him ", only in desperate times, but if we were in peaceful times, I would say rest for a week, but we are not in peaceful times; we are in desperate times and these desperate times are troubled so you may prepare for battle now." Eohdor turns to Ladel and says, "Great Ladel, walk with me to my Throne Room." the Grand Griffin Eohdor and the Great Sprite Ladel get up and walk to the Throne Room. They stand in the middle of the Pillar Throne. The Grand Griffin stamps his Mighty Paw, and a Gold and Silver Key appear. Meanwhile, in the Grand Griffin's Pillar Realm. A Marble Plinth in the shape of a Key appears before the Four Crowns. Nivea says to them, "Quick, you three, I have an idea. Grab your Trinkets and place them on the Plinth." Nivea places her Sword on the Plinth, Tresel places her Sandals on the Plinth, Stin places her Escutcheon on the Plinth, and Sastia places her Jewel on the Plinth. There is a thundery raw as the Plinth shakes, and four Suits of Silver and Gold Armour appear, each with a Feather on the Helmet, a shiny Sword, an impenetrable Escutcheon and impenetrable shining Armour. Nivea says to the group, "I think we should call the Grand Griffin to an audience." in the Throne Room, each of the four Marble Pillars shifts as the Four Crowns appear on each of them. The Grand Griffin holding the Key and standing in front of the Great Sprite Ladel, says s "Nivea, Tresel, Sastia, Stin, what are you doing."

Nivea tells him, "we have learnt our lesson Grand Griffin Eohdor." Tresel says, "we have read the Book of Ninarphay through and through." Stin says, "we understand now." Sastia says, "we won't do it again, Grand Griffin, sorry." The Monarchs repeatedly call in unison, "Sorry!"

Eohdor says, "I don't believe you." Nivea tells him, "we have increased our Powers as High Lords." Tresel says, "we are wiser and stronger." Stin says, "we are almost like Sages." Sastia says, "We want to help." They repeat in unison, "yes, we can help, we can help." The Grand Griffin shouts, "silence; over the past six weeks, Ninarphay has changed, and so has my opinion of you. I will consider your proposition, but I can't promise you freedom yet."

The Four Crowns say to the Grand Griffin. "thank you, Grand Griffin." The Four Crowns move their Faces from the exterior of the Plinths, and the Marble Plinths revert to their standard shape. The Grand Griffin turns to Ladel with the Key and begins to speak to her. He says, "Ladel, those four Ninarphaians you met with across my Lands, are High Classed Guardians who have been secretly trained for a battle like this. They have been assigned to Protect the Portal Keys.

This Key I'm giving you connects to six other Keys and has the power to permanently Lock away a Portal."

Ladel asks, "so what is my mission?" The Grand Griffin Eohdor tells her, "your mission is to find and locate those Ninarphaians, collect their Sacred Keys and with their help seal away the Portal."

Ladel asks, "why didn't you ask me to do this before?" The Grand Griffin Eohdor tells her, "it is only possible to seal a Portal once it is opened." Ladel says, "I see you can only close a Door forcefully if it is open." The Grand Griffin says, "Exactly. Once the Portal opens, we fight the enemy retreat, then seal the Gateway Portal to Transzalore." Ladel says, "I understand." Ladel suits up, straps on her Sword and exits the Sky Castle. Setting out on her quest to find the Four Guardians and their Sacred Keys.

CHAPTER 2

THE GREAT SPRITES QUEST

The Great Sprite Ladel arrives at Guardian Witch Zilley's House; as she is about to knock on the Door, Zilley's Door flies open, and Zilley says, "come in, Great Sprite Ladel. I was cooking Breakfast; it's your Favourite!" Ladel says, "my Favourite!" Zilley

says, "yes, your Favourite Curry!" Ladel says, "Curry for Breakfast!" Zilley says, "why not? This is a Curry House, and some Curries are meant to be eaten for Breakfast!" Ladel comes Clean and gets straight to the point. "listen, Zilley, I know you are the Guardian of one of the Sacred Keys. Grand Griffin has sent me on a Quest. To find the six Guardians of the Sacred Keys and seal away the evil doers of Transzalore from the Realm of Ninarphay."

Zilley say's "okay, let's put the Curry in the Bag and find the others. I am sure they will appreciate my cooking." Ladel asks, "where is the Key." Zilley taps her shoes together twice. The Key appears around her Neck. She then said, "let's go!" the pair left with the Key, Bag of Curry and a Sheaf of Tools.

Meanwhile, in Transzalore, Dark Lord Zenith gathers his Generals and Armies along with his five High Powered Nobles. Dark Lord Zenith Ogre King, leader of three Armies of Transzalore, Dark Lord Hogmass Sprite King 2nd highest Power and Ruler of Transzalore five Army Commander, Dark Lord Nobi Wizard King 5th highest Power and Ruler in Transzalore, Dark Elf Sheila Elf Queen, 6th highest Power and Ruler of Transzalore, Umi HaemoVampire King of Transzalore, 9th highest Power and Ruler of Transzalore.

They meet in Dark Lord Nobi's Counsel Room. Dark Lord Nobi and Dark Lord Zenith go over the plan of attack. Dark Lord Nobi lays down nine Maps of Ninarphay on the Table. He says to the Nobles, "we have nine Ninarphay Portal Keys, enough to get all our Armies through." He points to a Part of the Map and says, "we enter Ninarphay through the Portal hotspot of Ninarphay Forest on the Border of the Griffin Lands. There we will meet with resistance from Eohdor and other Pantheon Leaders. Dark Lord Zenith will remain in that area until the End of the battle in search of his four Crowns. The rest of our four Armies shall march on. "Dark Elf Sheila will march on the Phoenix Lands. We will begin to take over from the Blue River Phoenix and the Dragon Lord.

Our forces will march through Grand Tengu and Queen Tigers Kingdom Realms, where we shall spellbind and subdue the Enemy.

Count Umi will march on the Queen Bear and Blue Turtle Land, defeating and imprisoning the Pantheon and their Leaders. Finally, Hogmass will march on the

Queen witch and Grand Lord Reaper Lands defeating their Armies and imprisoning the Pantheon Leaders."

The Oni King is in his Throne Room with Delores and Nafrayer on either side. Hiethrieit enters and tells him, "my Sister and her Counsel are preparing to march on Ninarphay." The Oni King responds, "I know I saw the report this Morning!" Hiethrieit asks, "What are we going to do about this?" The Oni King tells her "wait here! My Oni Clan and I will visit them. They are no match for us together, no matter how powerful their rating is. I am sure we can persuade them to stand down." The Oni King goes to his Plinth and uses a commune spell to order his Clan Members of Oni Heritage to appear. One by one, five Oni Kings Clan Members begin appearing. First, his Brother Oni, Earl of the clear.

Conscience, second Oni Earl of the Good Mind, third Oni Count of the Resolute Eyes, fourth Oni Marquis of the Strong Heirs and finally, Oni Lord of the Good Nature. They open a Portal to the Dark Lord Zeniths Castle and enter freely. They walk past the many Infantries and arrive at Dark Lord Nobi's Counsel Chamber.

The Oni King exclaims to Dark Lord Nobi, "Dark Lord Nobi, stop this insanity now. I cannot allow you to invade Ninarphay." Hogmass turns to Nobi and says, "how are you going to handle this." Dark Lord Nobi tells them, "I've been crafting a spell to confuse the Oni King for years. The Elixir is in the Halls of this Castle and is designed specifically for him and his Clan." Zenith asks, "When will it work?" Nobi tells him, "It's starting to kick in." the Oni King, believing that Nobi is starting a fight, waves his Hands in the Air and then sits down. He repeats the same sentence five times, and all his Clan Members agree. Hogmass exclaims to the Counsel, "move out!" they all leave the Counsel Room and assemble the five Armies to move through the nine. Portals.

CHAPTER 3

THE INVASION BEGINS

The Grand Griffin is in his Courtyard gathering his Army. He gets called to his Counsel Room, where a magical image of the Blue River Phoenix is waiting. The Grand Griffin says to the Blue River Phoenix, "are your Legions ready? The nine Portals are opening, and the invasion is beginning." The Blue River Phoenix tells him, "my Legions are ready. I'll warn the rest of the Pantheon. Farewell Eohdor Grand Griffin of the Grand Pantheon Ninarphay."

The Grand Griffin suits in his Armour in the Throne Room. The four Monarchs beg again, "free us, Grand Griffin; we promise to uphold Justice and Harmony." The Grand Griffin tells them, "it's your fault this War began in the first place!" The four Monarchs exclaim, "we're sorry!" the Grand Griffin exits the Castle and marches his Army to the front of the Castle.

The five Armies of Transzalore march through the Portal and stand in Ninarphay Forest. The Grand Griffin Eohdor Army is outmatched twelve to one. The battle begins, and the Grand Griffin fights. The Grand Griffins Legion is soon pushed back into the

Castle. The Grand Griffins Legions are depleted, and the five Armies march on. The Grand Griffin Eohdor is cornered in his Throne Room by Dark Lord Zenith and his first Infantry. The Grand Griffin appears weak and beaten, unable to stand, limped and falls to the Floor. The Grand Griffin crawls to his Throne Perch where he gets up and, with the last of his Strength. The four Plinths spin, and the four Crowns are released from there in full Magical Armour with their Swords. "by the Heaven Scrolls of the Sages and the Elders of the Heavenly Sky, from this day forward, my Sword is meant for the ones Deservedness of I, the Justice in my Heart is Pure and will never harm the Innocent". Nivea swings her Sword at five of Dark Lord Zenith's 25 Infantry Trolls. Tresel standing High and Mighty proclaims. " by the Wisdom of the Grand Sages and the Heavenly Scrolls I shall hold Honour in my Heart and ensure all is well as the Power Bearer of a Region.

Continent". Tresel swings her Sword at five of the twenty-five Troll Lords of Dark Lord Zeniths' first Infantry. Stin steps forward with Guile and presence and says. "by the Infinite Wisdom of the Grand Sages who have ascended to the Heavenly Skies and the Sage Scrolls they Bequeathed us with I Promise to Love and Protect all in my Society who do the righteous thing and have Pure and Good Honour". Stin swings her Sword at five of the twenty-five Troll Lords. Sastia steps forward with Power and Might, clenching her Wooden Staff in her hands; she says with Great Courage and Conviction. "From this day forward, I will never again take Hard-Work and self Preservation for Granted. Grace is from within. The Troll Lord Infantry are soon defeated, and the four

Crowns stand before Dark Lord Zenith, the Ogre Lord and his first Company of Ogres. Nivea says to them, "since we last met me, my Sisters, I have grown exponentially in Class Status and Power". Dark Lord Zenith says, "it doesn't matter. You belong to me. Now come Home ". Tresel exclaims, "Make us"! A Great battle between Dark Lord Zenith, the four Crowns, and the

five Ogre Troll Lords. Sastia breaks off with her newly crafted Spirit Powers and uses the Power of her Staff to compel and defeat the five Ogre Troll Lords as the other three battle against Dark Lord Zenith. Tresel exclaims to Dark Lord Zenith, "give up; you have no chance of defeating four Grand Sages of High Lord Regency". The battle rages, and they each fight to Defend the Ninarphaian way.

Ladel and Zilley visit the Guardian Banshee Warrior Shila in her Taverns. Just as they enter, they notice several Army Legions marching toward them. They enter Shila's Tavern in a hurry and sigh of relief; as they enter Guardian, Shila asks, "what is wrong, Ladel"? Ladel answers, "we must act right away. The Legions of Transzalore are marching on Ninarphay"! Guardian Shila replies, "does the Grand Griffin deem it"? Ladel Tells her, "yes, he does". The Banshee Guardian responds, "wait here one minute". Shila goes into her Underground Store Room through a Secret compartment under her Table on the Floor and retrieves a Crystal Wand. The Crystal Wand glows bright green, and Guardian Banshee Shila tells the two Warriors, "all clear"! Shila quickly returns to her Underground Store Room with a golden Dagger with two Red Gems on the Handle and presents it to Ladel. Ladel asks, "what is this"? Shila remarks, "this is the second golden Key". Shila then presses on the two Gems and whispers an Incantation into the Dagger. A Portal opens, and the Dagger reforms into a Key Sheila, "this Portal should lead us to the third Key". They walk through the Portal and emerge in Dwarf Guardian Bifered Forgers Chamber. Guardian Dwarf Biffered is fast asleep with a bottle of Gin at his Bedside. He is snoring tightly and grasping onto a Forgers Hammer. Ladel pours Gin over his Head and exclaims, "wake up"! Bifered awakes, and Ladel tells him, "it is time the Grand Griffin has deemed that you join me on my Quest to banish the Dark Lords of Transzalore back to their wake"! Bifered bangs his Hammer in the Centre of the Forgers Chambers Talisman shaped Floor, and it turns into a Portal Key. A Portal opens, and the team of Guardians walk through it.

CHAPTER 4

THE GUARDIAN'S FINAL EXPEDITION FOR NINARPHAY

the four Guardians walk through the Portal Gate and are greeted by a Giant holding a Chopping Blade.

The Giant shouts at them, "what are you doing here," Ladel explains, "We have been sent here by the Pantheon of Ninarphay Ninarphay is in Danger, and we need the help to restore Order and return the Dark Lords, and their Armies to their Kingdom wakes. will you help us" the Giant tells them show me the Nature of there assault, and I will see what can be done. Zilley throws her Wand to the Ground, and in the Centre of the Floor, a projection opens up. The forecast displays the problems apparent with Ninanphay. Trolls march, eating pedantically, invading Shops and Kiosks, stealing Food and generally acting snobbish. The Grand Giant then tells them. "place all your Weapons on that Plinth, and together we will ensure the Laws of Ninarphay result in Order and Harmony" the Guardians place their Weapons on the Table, and the Giant, with his Hammer, bangs on the Table with Power and Astuteness. An immense glow appears over the Area, and soon a Portal Void begins to plume the Trolls into a Vortex. Out of Ninarphay, they are all transported back to their Lands, and all is well in Ninarphay again. the Giant turns to the Guardians and says. "okay, now you can go back to your Lands."

In Ninarphay, the Ninarphains celebrate victories. They hold a gathering at their respective Grand Castles of the individual Pantheon Leaders. They Drink, Laugh and Generally be Merry.

THE END

Printed in the United States
by Baker & Taylor Publisher Services